THE LAST STAND

THE
JUNIOR NOVEL

HarperCollins®, ☞®, and HarperKidsEntertainment™
are trademarks of HarperCollins Publishers.
X-Men: The Last Stand: The Junior Novel
Marvel, X-Men and all related character names and the distinctive likeness thereof are trademarks of
Marvel Characters, Inc. and are used with permission. Copyright © 2006 Marvel Characters, Inc.
All rights reserved.
www.marvel.com
© 2006 Twentieth Century Fox Film Corporation.
Printed in the United States of America.
No part of this book may be used or reproduced in any manner whatsoever without
written permission except in the case of brief quotations embodied in critical articles and reviews.
For information address HarperCollins Children's Books, a division of HarperCollins Publishers,
1350 Avenue of the Americas, New York, NY 10019.
www.harperchildrens.com
Book design by John Sazaklis
Library of Congress catalog card number: 2006920606
ISBN-10: 0-06-082208-2—ISBN-13: 978-0-06-082208-8
1 2 3 4 5 6 7 8 9 10
❖
First Edition

THE LAST STAND

THE
JUNIOR NOVEL

Adapted by Danny Fingeroth
Based on a Motion Picture Screenplay
written by Simon Kinberg & Zak Penn

HarperKidsEntertainment
An Imprint of HarperCollinsPublishers

1985.

The blue Mercedes sedan rolled swiftly down Thunderbird Lane. The leafy branches of the trees on either side of the road created a majestic covering for the quiet suburban street.

"This is it, Erik," Charles Xavier said, pointing from the car's front passenger seat. "Seventeen sixty-nine Thunderbird Lane."

The Mercedes glided to a halt in front of the Cape Cod–style house.

"I still don't know why we're here," Erik Lensherr

said. "Couldn't you just make them say yes?"

Xavier climbed out of the car and stood on the sidewalk.

"Of all people," he said, "I would expect you to understand my feelings about the misuse of power."

A small smile crept onto Erik's face. He and Charles had had this same conversation count- less times over the years. It was this very topic that threatened their often-strained friendship.

"Yes, I know," Erik said. "Power corrupts, and all that. When will you stop lecturing me?"

"When you start listening," Xavier retorted. The two men walked toward the front door.

"We're not really going to have to meet every one of them in person, are we?" Erik asked. He enjoyed baiting Charles like this.

Xavier's eyes narrowed as he looked at his old friend. "No. This one is special."

"Aren't they all?" Erik responded in a sarcastic tone.

Inside the suburban home, John and Elaine Grey were reading a brochure for the School for Gifted

Youngsters. They had read it so many times they knew its contents by heart. But something about reading it again and again made them feel better about the decision they had made.

"I just know she'll be happy there," Elaine said.

John was less optimistic. "I don't know if she'll be happy anywhere. Why would they do any better with her than we have?" he asked.

The knock on the door startled them both, even though they had been expecting it.

John opened the door. "Welcome, gentlemen," he said. "I'm so glad you came to get her. We worry about her when she travels alone."

"Your school looks wonderful," Elaine chimed in, trying to sound upbeat. "What a beautiful campus!"

"But what about her illness?" John asked.

"Illness?" Erik asked, taken aback.

"Now, John," Elaine said, "let's hear what these men have to say."

"You think your daughter is sick, Mr. Grey?" Erik asked. As he spoke, a silver picture frame on the wall behind John started to shake. Xavier shot a glance at Erik. He calmed down—and the frame stopped moving.

"The point of the school is to help children like your daughter," Erik said. "Can we speak to her alone?"

"Of course," Elaine said.

"Jean," she called, "please come downstairs ... if you're feeling up to it. There are some people here who'd like to meet you."

As if she had known her presence would be requested, thirteen-year-old Jean Grey was already starting down the steps from the second floor. When she reached the landing, her parents quickly rose from their seats and moved toward the kitchen, almost as if they were afraid to be in the same room with her. Jean seemed to enjoy this fact.

"We'll leave you, then," John said.

Walking confidently across the living room, the striking redhead sat down in a chair directly across from her visitors. She stared at them, especially Charles, as if daring them to speak to her.

Suddenly, she straightened in her chair. Xavier was indeed speaking to her—but not with his voice. She heard his thoughts in her mind.

"It's very rude of you, you know, to read my thoughts, or Mr. Lensherr's, without permission," Xavier scolded her telepathically.

Jean's eyes widened—then narrowed just as suddenly. "How did you know . . . ?" she asked, keeping the conversation on the mental plane.

"We are mutants," Xavier replied. "Like you."

A third telepathic voice entered the conversation: Erik Lensherr's. "Did you think you were the only one of your kind, girl?" he queried.

"I doubt you are like me," Jean responded, casually gesturing toward the street with one hand.

Xavier and Erik looked out the window. Across the street, a slim elderly man wearing pink golf trousers was watering his lawn with a garden hose. Suddenly, the water coming out of the nozzle started flowing *up*! The neighbor stared in shock. When he let go of the hose, the upward water flow continued. The hose danced around the lawn like a charmed snake.

Then, one by one, every car on the street outside rose a good ten feet into the air. Jean smiled. She was certain they had never seen anything like *this*.

And as the finale to this very strange show, a manual lawnmower rose up from a nearby lawn. The portly man who had been pushing it tumbled off into a row of manicured hedges.

Standing at the window, Erik put his hand on his friend's shoulder. "Oh, Charles, I *like* this one."

Xavier did not respond. He turned to face Jean.

"You have more power than you can imagine," Charles said silently. "The question is . . . will you control that power?"

Jean again gestured toward the street with an almost arrogant wave of her hand. Surely she had made it clear that she controlled her power.

Charles looked intently at the girl. He concentrated and focused his own energy. Jean was fighting back. It was a battle of two enormous wills.

Finally, Jean's features relaxed.

The cars crashed down onto the street. The hose and mower resumed their normal operation. Xavier stared at her. He spoke his next words aloud. "I ask again. Will you control that power, Jean—or will it control you?"

✳✳✳✳✳✳

1995.

The penthouse apartment of the Worthington family was known far and wide for its opulence. At this moment, outside one particularly luxurious bathroom, the elder Warren Worthington was uncharacteristically losing his cool. He banged repeatedly on the locked door.

"Warren," he shouted. "What's going on in there? Are you okay?"

"Nothing's going on," a voice from inside said. "I'm fine. I'll be right out," Warren Worthington III assured him. But the tone of the youngster's voice made it clear he was *not* fine.

"Come on, Warren, it's been an hour! Open this door!" the elder Worthington demanded.

"One sec," his son pleaded. "I'm almost finished." Sweat dripped down the twelve-year-old's face as he hurriedly jammed a handful of items into a drawer. The items included rubbing alcohol, cotton balls, gauze, and a set of gleaming kitchen knives.

Suddenly, with a powerful heave of his shoulder,

Worthington Sr. broke the lock. The door swung open. "You're finished *now*!" he barked.

He was not prepared for what he found inside.

The porcelain sink was spattered with red. The boy's blood was everywhere. Warren Kenneth Worthington III was wounded and in shock. But the strangest thing was that a cloud of white feathers was drifting to the floor.

The older Worthington felt sick.

Warren Worthington III had been trying to remove the wings that were growing from his back.

"Not *you*, son," Warren Sr. whispered.

"I'm sorry, Dad," was all the boy could say before he collapsed to the floor. He lay there like a fallen angel.

2

Alcatraz Island, off the coast of San Francisco, was once the home of a famous prison called the Rock. For many years, the old prison building was a tourist attraction. More recently, the structure had become the headquarters of Worthington Labs. Warren Worthington Sr. had spent the last decade assembling and creating the finest facility of its kind.

Alcatraz was now a center for mutant research.

In a state-of-the-art lab inside the former prison, Dr. Kavita Rao was a model of single-minded concentration as she went about her work. She carefully clipped the fingernails of a child seated before her. Just as carefully, she placed the clippings in a sterile glass container.

The child had wide blue eyes and a shaved head. He was called "Leech." While the name was not a compliment, it was not an insult either. It was a description of a special ability he had—a mutant ability.

Whether that ability was a blessing or a curse, no one could yet say.

Smoke rose from the rubble of what had once been a vibrant city street. Fires still danced in the windows of some of the smoldering buildings. Clearly something terrible had occurred here.

Suddenly a small flame burst into view. As it moved through the darkness, its flickering light glinted off the eyes of the man holding the match. He moved the flame to the end of his cigar stub and puffed until it was lit. Explosions were going off all around him as jagged pieces of metal shrapnel streaked past. But the man remained intent on enjoying his smoke. He wasn't going to let anyone ruin his moment, not even his agitated teammate.

"Aside from the fact that that's disgusting, Wolverine—it's also making us into targets," Rogue lectured him.

A metallic hand attached to a metallic arm grabbed her by the elbow. "Being a target is fine, Rogue," Colossus said to her, "so long as you're a target who can withstand being hit."

Rogue's skin transformed as she, too, became a creature of living metal. Her mutant ability to absorb the qualities of other beings had kicked into play. Pieces of debris bounced off her, as they did off of Colossus.

"Thank you, darlin'," Rogue said. "You okay? I didn't drain too much of your power, did I?"

Colossus, also known as Peter Rasputin, started to answer when a loud crashing sound was heard in the distance.

"It's getting closer," Colossus said.

There was another explosion, and a jagged piece of shrapnel zoomed between him and Rogue. The metal fragment landed squarely in Wolverine's cheek. Still puffing on his cigar, he popped a foot-long metal claw from the back of his wrist. Calmly, he used the claw to pick the shrapnel from his face.

The wound bled slightly, than healed itself completely. No matter how many times they saw it, Wolverine's ability to heal himself never failed to amaze Colossus and Rogue.

"Don't try this at home, kids," Wolverine, also known as Logan, quipped. "Stogies and shrapnel—they'll both kill you if you don't have a mutant healing factor."

"Thanks for that very special public service message," Rogue said. She turned to Colossus. "How long do we have?" she asked him.

"Two minutes, tops."

"I'm away a few days and the whole world falls apart, eh?" Logan said. "So . . . do you want to just stand here and be a target?"

Rogue pointed off into the distance. "If we get to that bunker," she said, "we're clear."

"Let's go," Logan said calmly.

Suddenly a howling wind began to blow from the far side of a nearby hill. But the gusts weren't created by nature, they came from a mutant called Storm. She was flying toward Logan and the others, carried aloft by the air currents she had created.

Storm suddenly spied danger from the opposite direction.

"Kitty! Bobby! Incoming!" Rogue shouted.

Bobby Drake—code-named "Iceman"—saw the speeding missile, and started to construct an ice shield. He concentrated his mutant power as best he could, but it wasn't working fast enough. The rocket was coming closer and closer.

Kitty grabbed her icy companion and closed her eyes.

The rocket passed harmlessly through them and exploded on the side of a nearby building. The structure instantly crumbled to dust.

"You okay?" Kitty asked.

"Yeah," Bobby replied. "You?"

"A little dusty," she said. Bobby reached out and brushed off her shoulder. Their eyes met, and the glance lasted for a second.

"Only a quarter mile to the end," Bobby said awkwardly.

"Right," replied Kitty. "Follow my lead."

Bobby smiled as Kitty took his hand and they continued on.

Rogue was happy that her friends were unharmed, but she couldn't help feeling jealous. Other people—mutants and humans alike—could touch each other. They didn't have to worry about absorbing other people's energy to the point of killing them.

She especially hated that she couldn't touch her boyfriend, Bobby Drake. She loved him, and he felt the same way about her. But what boy would stay involved with someone he couldn't ever touch? Especially with someone as cute as Kitty Pryde around?

Rogue suddenly hated herself for even thinking such petty thoughts right now. There were matters of life and death at hand.

As Bobby and Kitty made their way to the bunker, Kitty's phasing power allowed rockets to continue to pass through them harmlessly.

"Keep moving!" Logan called to them.

The X-Men were now united. Their moment of truth was at hand. Wolverine puffed away on his cigar, as cool and calm as ever.

"This isn't a game," Storm said, frowning at him. She checked her palm-device map. "We've got one minute and thirty seconds left. Time to get serious."

"I'm always serious, Storm," Wolverine said. "For instance, I seriously believe we're in big trouble."

As Wolverine spoke, the crashing sounds grew louder—and closer—than before. The ground shook with each terrifying crash. A giant mechanical creature was bearing down on them. The thing must have been a hundred feet tall.

"Kids, meet the Sentinel," Wolverine said.

As the creature approached, the X-Men slowly backed away from it. Suddenly, they found their way blocked by what seemed like a mountain of metal.

The Sentinel continued to advance, its massive shadow falling over them.

3

Wolverine put out his cigar. He spoke to Colossus, but kept his eyes on the advancing iron giant.

"How's your pitching arm?" Wolverine asked.

"As good as ever, considering baseball is not my homeland's national pastime," said Colossus.

"Mine, either," Wolverine said. "Hockey's what excites a Canuck like me! But I still say nobody does a fastball special like us. You ready?"

"*Da,*" Colossus, the Russian-born mutant, replied.

"Then let's do it."

Colossus grabbed Wolverine in his metal arms, then reared back and unleashed him in the direction of the Sentinel's head.

As he soared upward, Wolverine's claws—three on each side—popped from the backs of his hand with a distinctive *snikt*.

Wide-eyed, the other X-Men watched. "Look out below!" Wolverine cried.

An instant later, a huge object was falling toward the mutants. Sparks were shooting out of it in a strangely beautiful display. The X-Men scattered out of the way as it hit the ground with a metallic crash. The Sentinel's head rolled toward them, coming to a halt in front of Storm. Its sparking eyes went black.

"That serious enough for you, Storm?" Wolverine called out as he landed back on his feet. A few moments later, the rest of the robot's body hit the ground, crushing everything that lay in its path.

A clanging alarm suddenly pierced the night. Was another enemy attacking?

All at once, the setting changed. What had

been a terrifying urban battle zone was now a large, nondescript room. Aside from the mutants, the room was completely empty. There was no hint of the fires, the rubble; certainly no sign that a Sentinel had ever been there.

"Workout's over! Good session, people," Wolverine called out. Aside from the mutants, everything had been a holographic projection in an indoor practice area called the Danger Room. "I'm hungry," he said. "Who wants pizza?"

Wolverine turned to Colossus. "Hey, tin man," he said with a smile, "you throw like a girl . . . overhand."

"I just didn't want to hurt you, old man," Colossus replied. He was smiling, too. Their fast-ball special was always fun—and effective.

As the team emerged from the Danger Room, Storm approached Wolverine.

"What was that?" Storm asked. There was an edge in her voice.

"A Danger Room session," Wolverine replied calmly.

"You know what I mean," Storm said. "It was supposed to be a defensive exercise. *Defensive.*"

"The best defense is a good offense," Wolverine said. "Or is it good offense is the best defense? I always get those mixed up." He was enjoying this. He liked messing with Storm.

She was in his face now. "These kids need to learn to work together, to follow an objective. They don't need your showboating."

"Hey, I'm just the sub, Storm. If you've got a problem, talk to Cyclops."

Scott Summers' room was in another wing of the X-Mansion. The lights were out and the shades were drawn. Scott—code-named Cyclops—was in no mood to deal with anyone. Unshaven, in rumpled clothes, there was little trace of the cocky X-Men team leader he used to be.

Scott was seeing things. Or specifically, one thing—a place called Alkali Lake. In his vision, he saw reeds by the side of the lake. And in the reeds lay a woman.

Real or false, Scott knew he had to follow this vision.

He grabbed his duffel bag and left the room. The hall lights glinted off his ruby-quartz sunglasses. But the shades couldn't disguise his intensity of purpose.

"I'm fine," Rogue insisted. "Really."

"You don't seem fine to me," Iceman replied. "You're avoiding me. What's wrong?"

"What's *wrong*?" she repeated. She couldn't hide her sorrow and her anger any longer. "What's wrong is that I can't touch my boyfriend without killing him. Other than that, I'm wonderful."

The couple was walking through the halls of the School for Gifted Youngsters. In rooms all around them, students were doing the most amazing things. But no one was amazed by any of it. In this school for "gifted youngsters"—what the public commonly called "mutants"—the amazing was commonplace.

Despite himself, Iceman became defensive. "That's not fair," he said, "Have I put any pressure on you?"

"You're a guy, Bobby," she said, her emotion spilling out. "There's only one thing on your mind."

Iceman tried to steer the conversation elsewhere.

"We're part of the team now, Rogue. We have responsibilities."

"Yeah, I've heard this speech before," she snapped. They had reached her room. Rogue opened the door and entered, then slammed it shut in Iceman's face.

In the oak-paneled front hall of the mansion, other tempers were flaring.

"We were looking for you downstairs," Wolverine said.

"What do you care about me?" Cyclops shot back.

"I had to cover for you again, for starters," Wolverine said.

"I didn't ask you to," Cyclops replied. He was distracted, his mind on other things.

"No, *the Professor* did," Logan replied.

There was an awkward silence. Wolverine tried to reach out to his teammate. "I know how you feel."

"Don't," Cyclops snapped.

Wolverine kept going: "When Jean died . . ."

"DON'T!" Cyclops shouted.

Wolverine was going to make his point, no matter what. "Maybe it's time to move on."

Cyclops opened the front door. He paused a second, and turned back to face Wolverine. "Not everyone heals as fast as you," Cyclops said.

He walked through the door and over to his motorcycle. He jumped on the starter and revved up the bike. In a cloud of exhaust fumes, the engine roaring, he was off the school grounds in seconds.

4

The young assistant rushed into the White House office of the Secretary of Mutant Affairs. Inside, a blue-furred mutant was hanging from the light fixture.

"You're late for your meeting with the President, sir," the assistant said.

Despite the fur that covered his agile body, the creature was wearing a finely tailored suit and a tasteful—but not too tasteful—tie. He folded his copy of the economics journal he was reading and dropped it onto his desk.

With a showy flourish, he spun himself in the air and landed on the carpeted floor of his office. Adjusting his tie and glasses, and popping a breath mint in his mouth, Dr. Henry "Hank" McCoy—also know as Beast—dashed out the door.

McCoy sped through the corridors of the White House, creating a wind that caused papers to fly out of the hands of startled secretaries and interns.

" 'Scuse me, pardon me," he said as he passed them. He caught a stack of papers as they flew out of one intern's hands. He neatly put them back together, handed them to her, and then continued on.

Finally, he glided through an imposing door marked with the presidential seal.

"You're late, Hank," the President of the United States said.

"Sorry, Mr. President. Traffic on the beltway."

Dr. Bolivar Trask, Director of Homeland Security, was seated next to the President. Several other important officials were also in the room. Something big was going on.

"I'll let Trask bring you up to date," the President said.

Hank felt as if Trask was angry with him, even though they barely knew each other. But Hank was a mutant, and that was all the reason Trask needed to hate him.

"We almost had Lensherr himself," Trask said.

"You had Magneto?" McCoy replied, impressed.

"As I said, we *almost* had him," Trask continued. It pained him to have to admit this failure. "He slipped away. But we were able to capture his colleague Mystique, breaking into F.D.A. headquarters."

"Why would Magneto care about the Food and Drug Administration?" McCoy asked, genuinely puzzled. "Is he worried about the fat content in his burgers?"

"Do you know who she was impersonating?" the President asked.

"Elvis?" McCoy quipped. No one laughed.

"Me!" Trask shouted, slamming his fist on the table.

McCoy had to stifle a laugh. "She's a shape-shifter. She can do that."

"Not anymore she can't," Trask said, triumphantly. "We've got her."

Hank knew Mystique was bad news. Her capture was a good thing. Still, he hated Trask's smug attitude. "You think your four walls can hold her?" Hank asked.

"Mutants adapt," Trask said. "We humans can, too. They develop new powers, we develop new prisons. We'll be a step ahead from now on."

While this meeting was going on, a meeting of another sort was taking place: an interrogation. It was being held in a windowless room, where the only light came from a blinding spotlight aimed at a woman's face.

The F.B.I. agent spoke in a soft, menacing voice. "This can go hard or easy, Raven."

"I don't answer to my slave name," Mystique hissed at him.

The agent remained calm. "It's the name on your birth certificate. Raven Darkholme. Or is *he* your family now?"

The strangely beautiful woman with blue-scaled skin betrayed no emotion. "I don't know who you're referring to," she said. As she spoke, she transformed into an exact twin of the man questioning her. This made the agent nervous, but he tried not to show it.

"Are you playing games?" he asked. "Because I'm *not*. Where is Magneto?"

Mystique suddenly morphed into Magneto, standing tall and wearing a white prison outfit.

"I'm here, with us," Mystique replied, sounding exactly like Magneto.

"Tell me," the F.B.I. man continued, "is it worth enduring all we can do to you just to protect him?"

"You want to know where he is?" Mystique asked. She motioned for the agent to come closer, as if she had a secret to tell him, and she shape-shifted again.

He leaned toward her. He found it very troubling to be looking at himself. Suddenly, Mystique whipped her head forward, smashing it into his. The identical skulls slammed together with a harsh crack.

Mystique jumped up onto the table and pulled her legs up through her hand restraints. Cartwheeling off the table, Mystique moved toward the agent and started to strangle him with her hand restraints.

The F.B.I. agent staggered back in agony. Guards rushed into the room. As they subdued Mystique with multiple Taser blasts, she reverted to her blue-scaled self.

This bizarre episode had been witnessed on a computer monitor by Beast and the others in the White House meeting room. Trask switched off the monitor.

Hank spoke first. "Her capture will only provoke Magneto," he said.

Trask looked at Hank as if he were a fool. "Did you see what she did? See what we're dealing with?"

"All the more reason to be diplomatic," McCoy retorted. He was trying his best to hold back his anger. He had to stay cool and professional. He was a mutant. They weren't.

"You don't expect me to negotiate with these

people, do you?" the President asked.

"I thought that was why you appointed *me*, Mr. President," Hank replied.

"We'll see," the President said. "But believe it or not, I didn't call this meeting so we could watch mutant-reality-TV."

"Then why?" Hank asked.

The President handed Beast a folder stamped CLASSIFIED: TOP SECRET.

"It's the information that Mystique stole from the F.D.A. before we captured her," the President said. "We don't know how much of it she was able to get to Magneto."

Hank opened the folder and read its contents. His eyes grew wide. The more he read, the more shaken he became.

"My lord . . . is it viable?" Hank asked.

"Yes," the President responded flatly. "We just wanted you to know about it."

Hank suddenly realized where he stood: They wanted him to know. But they didn't want him to know in time to do anything about it. After all, you can trust a mutant—but only so far.

5

"Power, no matter how well-intentioned its wielder, corrupts," Charles Xavier said. "That is its nature."

Bright sunlight flooded the classroom at the School for Gifted Youngsters, where the Professor was teaching a class on mutant ethics.

The students had heard this lecture many times. Xavier didn't need his mind-reading abilities to know that some of them were quite bored with it. But he also knew that the lesson was one that had to be taught over and over before it sank in.

Kitty Pryde had heard this speech more times than she could remember. She agreed with it. Her experience as an X-Man had demonstrated its truth to her. *Still*, she thought, *a little conflict might kick things up a notch*.

"Professor," she said, "don't you think Magneto would say the same thing about you that you do about him? That *you* abuse *your* power?"

Xavier smiled. He knew what Kitty was up to. "I know for a fact that he *does* believe that, Kitty. That is why I force my students to sit through classes in ethics. Everyone, mutant and human alike, has to deal with either wielding power or being the object of it. . . . Or do you think I'm wrong?"

The mutants-in-training perked up as they saw signs of possible conflict. Kitty's plan was working.

"I might just phrase it differently," she replied. "I'd say that we're each on our own to figure out the right way to use our mutant powers."

"Interesting," Xavier replied. "Another way to phrase it would be: Is the power worth the responsibility? If you could rid yourselves of your mutant abilities, would you?" The students were clearly interested now. "So," Xavier continued, "what do the rest of you think?"

Hands shot up. The students were eager to chime in. But before Xavier could call on anyone, the bright sunlight that had been streaming into the room suddenly vanished. Dark clouds filled the sky and violent winds shook the windows.

Xavier's face darkened, too. He knew the cause of the sudden change in the weather. "We will have to pick up this discussion another day," he said. "Feel free to continue it amongst yourselves."

The professor turned his wheelchair around and rolled himself out of the classroom. He sped down the hall and out a side door. Looking up, he saw Storm gliding along the winds she had created.

She landed gracefully in front of the professor.

"The weather you bring always reflects your mood," the professor said. "What's bothering you?"

"My apologies, Professor," she said. Her eyes

cleared, and the sky became sunny again. Xavier had a calming presence on Storm.

"The same things trouble me that have been weighing on my mind for a while," Storm said. "But each day they grow harder to live with."

She walked closer to the professor and continued. "We have in office a president sympathetic to mutants. There's a mutant in his cabinet. Magneto is on the run. So, why are we still hiding?"

"We are not hiding," Xavier replied. "My students are vulnerable as they learn to use their powers. I have to protect them."

"The world will have to deal with us and we with it, Professor," Storm replied. "We can't be students forever."

"I stopped thinking of you as a student long ago, Storm," Xavier said. "In fact, I can imagine you taking over for me one day."

She was startled by this comment. "Me? What about Scott? Or Logan?"

"Scott has taken Jean's death so hard he is unable to think about anything else," Xavier responded. "And Logan's not interested."

"So I'd get the job because no one else wants it?" Storm asked.

"Not at all," the professor said. "But perhaps we should continue this discussion in my office." He wheeled himself back into the mansion, Storm walking by his side. They entered the building and continued to his office.

"Odd," Xavier said, "I don't remember leaving a light on." Closing his eyes, he did a mental scan. Then, with a sigh of relief, he opened the office door.

"Do make yourself at home, Dr. McCoy," Xavier said. "No reason to bother with a formality like asking if you could use my office."

Beast was perched on the back of the professor's desk chair. "My apologies, Professor. I thought you'd best hear my news in person, before the whole world finds out about it."

"What news?" Storm asked.

"For one thing, the government has Mystique," Hank replied. "She was in the process of stealing certain information from the F.D.A."

"And what was this information?" the professor asked.

"That's the other news," Beast said. "A major drug company has developed a mutant antibody—a way to suppress the mutant gene permanently. A cure for mutantcy, if you will."

"Since when is it a *disease*?" Storm asked. Her eyes were clouding over again.

"Since this guy got involved," Beast replied. He pressed a button on the professor's TV remote. An image appeared on an all-news network. The same report was being shown on almost every channel.

It was a broadcast from Alcatraz Island, where Warren Worthington Sr. was talking to a crowd of reporters.

"Thank you for coming," he said, smiling. "I've called you here to discuss the mutant problem."

"Mutants," he continued, "have been labeled saints and sinners. Monsters. But they are people just like us. Their affliction is nothing more than a disease, a corruption of healthy cellular activity."

Storm looked at the professor. She didn't like where this was heading.

"Finally," Worthington said, "there is hope! A

way to eradicate their suffering. After many years of experimentation, there is now ..."

"Here it comes," McCoy said.

". . . a cure," Worthington said triumphantly. "And Alcatraz will be the home to that cure."

"Ten to one," Hank said, "he's developed a mutant in the family."

6

"**C**ure?" Storm said with disgust, as if the word itself was poison. "There's nothing *to* cure! Who would want this cure? What kind of coward would take it just to fit in?"

"Avoiding persecution isn't cowardice, my dear," Beast said, less calmly than he would have liked. "Not all of us have such an easy time fitting in. *You* don't shed on the furniture."

"So you're saying you helped your friends in the government concoct this ... this thing?" Storm demanded.

"I had nothing to do with this," Beast replied. "Nor did the government. At least as far as I know."

Wolverine had entered the room. "And how much have they *allowed* you to know, Dr. McCoy?" he asked. "Not much, I bet. They're using you."

"And I'm using *them*," Beast countered. "Would you rather *not* have one of us on the inside?"

"*Are* you one of us?" Wolverine demanded. "Or only until you can use the cure on yourself? Maybe you'd like us to start a fund to buy you a dose."

"Don't lecture me, boy," Beast exploded. "I've been fighting for mutant rights since before you had claws."

"Enough! All of you!" Xavier exclaimed.

Rogue entered the room breathlessly. "Is it true?" she cried. "They can cure us?"

Storm's eyes narrowed to angry slits. "No. Because there's nothing *to* cure. There's *nothing* wrong with you."

Rogue looked down at her gloved hands. She could never forget that her gloves, in fact all of her clothes, were designed to make sure her skin would never accidentally come into contact with anyone else's.

Rogue wasn't so sure there was nothing wrong with her.

The flier nailed to the door of the abandoned theater said it all: COMMUNITY ACTION MEETING. OUR RESPONSE TO THE SO-CALLED CURE.

And on the bottom of the flier were scrawled the words: NO HUMANS ALLOWED.

Inside the theater, as in many places all over the world, the cure and what it meant was being debated by mutants.

A well-dressed, middle-aged mutant was standing on the stage. "Please sign your name to the e-mail sheet that's going around," he said, "so we can organize and deal with the issues."

A young woman in the orchestra section stood up. "I suggest we form committees to look into the legal and ethical issues," she said.

"The cure is voluntary," an earnest young mutant piped in. "There's no need to talk about extremes."

"I *strongly* disagree," boomed a voice from above.

A majestic, silver-haired mutant had spoken those words. He floated down from a balcony seat.

Magneto had come to the meeting.

"It is too late to organize," he continued. "Too late to form committees. They plan to exterminate us. The war has already begun."

The man who had once been Erik Lensherr effortlessly held himself aloft on waves of magnetic energy.

"I am looking for a few select members for my Brotherhood of Mutants," he continued. "If you feel my way is the correct path, please come speak to me."

With that, he floated through the crowd, and into the theater's lobby.

A few mutants followed him. They were pierced and tattooed and seemed to be there as a group. One of them had a tattoo in the shape of the Greek letter omega, which stood for "the end, the culmination." To mutants, it meant that they were the crowning result of human evolution, superior to humans.

"You talk tough," the woman with the tattoo said to Magneto. "But talk is cheap."

"The record is clear," he replied. "I do far more than talk. But what about you? What do *you* do besides talk, Ms....?"

"My name is Callisto," she said. "I have an ability the government would love, I'm sure."

Magneto raised an eyebrow. "And that would be what?" he challenged her.

"I can locate mutants anywhere," she said.

Magneto was clearly interested. "Well, Callisto," he smiled, "it so happens there is a missing mutant I'm quite *eager* to find."

7

The roar of Cyclops' motorcycle echoed across Alkali Lake. Something had pulled him here. Something impossible.

Cyclops brought the chopper to a halt a few yards from the lake. He got off the bike and walked to the water. The lake's surface was rippling, as if a breeze was passing over it. But the air was calm and still.

The water began to move more and more violently. Then, in a motion that defied all logic, it parted! And from the center of the newly formed void, a flicker of light appeared. He stared as the flicker grew brighter and brighter. Finally, it lit the entire lake and the surrounding area. And then the source of the light became visible, as a creature of pure, pulsing energy rose from the water's depths, hovering like a newborn star in the sky.

Cyclops watched as the star slowly descended. Still amazingly bright, it was glowing less intensely. It landed on the lake's surface, mere yards from where he stood.

He took a small step forward, straining to see what was at the center of the light. Then he stopped where he stood. Shock registered on his face and in every cell in his body.

"Jean …?" he whispered, both fearing and hoping that what he was seeing was really there.

He had watched his beloved Jean Grey sacrifice her life to save mankind. Her loss had devastated him and left him in a frail emotional state. He must be hallucinating. What else could it be?

Then the glow died down and he could see her clearly. It was Jean, reborn, standing before him.

The woman looked down at her limbs, her

skin. She seemed as stunned and disoriented as Cyclops.

"A dream ..." Cyclops mumbled. "This has to be a dream."

But when she looked up and her eyes met his, he knew he wasn't dreaming. Jean blinked a few times, slowly recognizing him. Memories came flooding back to her.

"Scott?"

There was only one voice like that. He had no doubt it was her. His lost love had impossibly returned to him.

He stepped toward her. "How ... how could you be back?"

Jean once again looked down at her body. "I don't know," she said.

Cyclops didn't care. All he knew was that his heart was suddenly lighter than it had been in months.

Jean strode onto the shore and stood on a rock. Scott swiftly closed the distance between them and took her in his arms. He held her close, hugging her tightly. Then he pulled back so they could look at each other.

Jean reached for his sunglasses. "Take these off," she said tenderly. "I want to look into your beautiful eyes."

Cyclops pulled back. Removing the glasses would leave his eyebeams unshielded. If his eyes were exposed for even an instant, the beams would destroy whatever—or whoever—was in their path.

Jean shook her head. She could sense her own power. "Trust me. I can control it. You won't hurt me."

Relaxing, Cyclops allowed Jean to remove the protective glasses. They came together for a kiss. As she had promised, her power was indeed enough to keep his lethal eyebeams in check.

And then, Jean started glowing again, with a pure, white energy that spread over and through her and everything around her. It caused Cyclops' skin to vibrate and shiver. He screamed as the energy overwhelmed him.

8

Charles Xavier cried out. He was experiencing psychic pain like none he had ever felt before.

All through the mansion, students reeled and cradled their heads as their teacher's agony passed through them.

Xavier had to know what had caused his pain. Sensing Xavier's suffering, Storm and Wolverine rushed downstairs into Xavier's office. "Take the jet to Alkali Lake," Xavier directed them. "Report everything you see."

The two X-Men raced to the underground hangar.

Minutes later, the school's basketball court started shaking, first mildly, then with more force. Students shooting hoops ran for the sidelines.

The court's asphalt surface split in two at the half-court line, the two halves sliding away to create a large opening. Seconds later, the *X-Jet* rose up gracefully through it.

As the craft flew through the skies, there was silence in the cockpit. Wolverine and Storm had no idea what to expect.

The jet landed in a clearing near Alkali Lake. Wolverine and Storm were out of the hatch before the plane had even come to a complete stop.

Wolverine saw something floating on the beach. The light glinted off it in a way that only ruby-quartz could reflect.

He had found Scott's sunglasses.

Wolverine popped out a claw and hooked the glasses onto it. He slipped them into his back pocket. But then his mutant senses detected another scent besides Cyclops', one that was shockingly familiar. His nostrils flared as he raced, full speed, in the direction the scent was coming from.

Storm ran behind him. "Be careful," she called. "It could be a trap." But he didn't hear her. He homed in on his target and shut out any other input.

Then Wolverine saw her.

Jean lay motionless among small rocks along the craggy shore of the lake.

Wolverine approached the body, barely breathing. Storm came up behind him and knelt down beside her sister mutant. "She's alive!" Storm exclaimed as she checked Jean's wrist for a pulse. "*Jean's alive!*"

Wolverine took the unconscious Jean in his arms and carried her back to the *X-Jet*. Storm followed. She knew that whatever happened, none of their lives would ever be the same.

"She suffers from what can loosely be termed a split personality," Xavier said.

He sat in the mansion's infirmary, his wheelchair pulled up close to where Jean was lying.

Wolverine paced impatiently around the examination room. Storm sat in a chair on the other side of Jean, across from the professor.

"Many years ago," Xavier continued, "when I first met Jean, I saw the potential she had. Potential to do great good—or great *harm*."

"You ever going to get to a point, Charlie?" Wolverine snapped. "Do you know something about how Jean came back? Or about that brain blast you got hit with?"

Xavier continued as if Wolverine hadn't interrupted. "I had to make a decision about that potential. Uncontrolled—or controlled by the wrong forces—her power could have been a menace. So I took action."

"You *did* something to her, Professor?" Storm shouted. "What? What did you *do*?"

Xavier looked at Jean. "I used my psychic abilities to block her awareness of her powers," he said. "In that way, I hoped, I could later help her control them.

"And I did help her. Her conscious side is Jean, always in control."

The professor paused, emotion choking

his voice. Wolverine glared at him with angry impatience.

The professor cleared his throat and went on. "However, the side of which she is unaware—the 'sleeping' side—is what I call 'the Phoenix.' It is pure instinct, filled with desire, with joy. And with rage.

"The Phoenix," he continued, "has somehow been let loose."

Xavier looked at Jean tenderly, tears welling in his eyes. "My task now is to re-cage the beast. I have to restore the psychic barriers I put in place when she was thirteen."

Wolverine stopped pacing and looked straight at Xavier. "So, Professor," he said, "you've decided the best way to make up for what you did to her in the past is to do it to her *again*? And until you're able to do that, you're keeping her unconscious? How could you do this to her?"

"She has to be controlled."

"Controlled? Or *cured*?" Wolverine snarled.

"You don't know what Jean is capable of," the professor replied.

"Maybe not, Professor. But I sure had no idea what *you* were capable of."

"I want her back as much as you do," Xavier said. "I had a terrible choice to make, and I chose the lesser of two evils."

Wolverine clenched his fists. "You sure?"

Sudden, overpowering rage shook Xavier. "I don't need to explain myself to you, Logan. I will do what needs to be done."

9

Dr. Rao had an important visitor: the Secretary of Mutant Affairs.

She and Henry McCoy entered Leech's Alcatraz room. It was all white, with only a few toys neatly tucked away. Instead of creating a feeling of normalcy, though, these items just made the situation even stranger. It was not a room in a normal home. And Leech was not a normal kid. Another child sat near him, playing a video game.

"This is Dr. McCoy," Rao said to the child.

"Hello," Leech said shyly.

"Hi there," Beast said. He reached an arm out to the boy.

As he did, the blue fur on his hand started to disappear, and his mutant hide began to turn into normal human skin.

For a moment, Beast was tempted to remain in Leech's presence. In a matter of minutes, he would no longer be a mutant. He would be "cured."

But Beast took a step back. This was not his path. The changes in his hand reversed themselves. Jimmy moved away from Leech as well, and as he walked away, webbing began to grow between his fingers and reptilian scales returned to his face.

"I think we should be going," he said. "Very nice to have met you, uh, Leech."

"Is that the best name you could come up with for him?" Beast asked Dr. Rao as they left the room.

"An odd question coming from someone who calls himself 'Beast,' " she replied. "But he actually seems to like the name."

"I see," Beast said. "Well, doctor, thank you for allowing me to meet him."

Beast had information now. The question

was, what would he do with it?

As he left the building, he passed a line of mutants. Some looked like normal humans, while others were quite strange looking. They had all come to get the cure.

But across the road, there were other mutants. "Mutants are beautiful!" they chanted. "The cure is a trap!" And they held signs with similar messages: THE CURE = MURDER. LOVE YOURSELF. MUTANT AND PROUD.

The mutant cure was a controversy that wasn't going away anytime soon.

Dr. Rao returned to her lab. The Worthingtons—father and son—were waiting for her there.

"Are you sure you want to do this?" she said to the elder Worthington.

"We have to," he replied. "People have to see how important this is to me."

His son was seated on an examination table. His wings, which had grown huge over the past ten years, were held in place by a complex harness. Grim-faced orderlies towered behind him.

"I'm proud of you for doing this, son," the older man said. He turned to Dr. Rao. "Let's begin," he said.

Dr. Rao filled a hypodermic needle with serum made from Leech's DNA. The serum was, of course, the cure.

"The transformation can be a little jarring," she said.

"Dad," the winged mutant said, "can we talk about this for a second? I *don't* want to do this."

"You'll be fine," his father replied. "Just calm down."

But the young man *wouldn't* calm down. He strained against the harness and jumped off the table. The orderlies grabbed him and tried to hold him down. But young Warren was fueled by anger, panic, and fear. They couldn't keep him still.

His father joined the orderlies. He held his son tightly. "Do it! Quickly!" he ordered the doctor.

Warren Worthington III thrashed more and more violently. The straps on his harness were stretching from his efforts, until, finally, they broke! The restraints broke into pieces and clat-tered to the floor.

Now free, Warren shoved the orderlies away. As he ran from them, a fluttering sound was heard, and then a snap, as if a whip had been cracked.

Warren Worthington III's wings unfurled!

It was a magnificent sight. For a moment, everyone else in the room was frozen. Even Warren's father could say or do nothing.

Then the moment was gone. "Warren … son … we discussed this. This is what you want."

"No," the winged youth replied, "it's what *you* want."

He turned to leave, but guards blocked the door. He spun around to face the lab's windows, tucking his wings behind him as he crouched.

"Warren! NO!" his father cried.

But there was no turning back for the young mutant. He leaped toward the windows. Then, shielding his face with his folded arms, he crashed through them.

The sound of shattering glass rang across the island. The mutants on the cure line and on the protest line looked up to see the source of the noise. Glass shards exploded out from the front of the building. And from the fragments, an *angel* flew.

Warren Worthington III soared gracefully over the crowd below. They watched with awe as he disappeared into the sky.

10

The President of the United States sat in a windowless prison cell.

"Sorry, Mr. President, you're not going anywhere," a guard seated nearby taunted him.

"My authority doesn't sway you?" the chief executive asked. "How about this, then?" And he turned into a cute little girl.

"You wouldn't keep a sweet, innocent thing like me in this cell, would you?" she asked.

"You ain't no sweet, innocent *nothin'*." The guard laughed. He was amused, even if he wasn't moved to action.

"Then how about *this*?" the girl said, and transformed herself into an exact duplicate of the guard.

"Good looking—but no dice." The guard smiled. "Face it, Mystique, you can make yourself look like my mom. Or an apple pie. You *still* ain't gettin' out of here."

POP!

The guard was on his feet in a flash. "What was that?" he cried.

"I didn't hear anything," Mystique said, although she clearly had. She reverted to her blue-scaled form, enjoying the guard's anxiety, eager for what she knew would be coming next.

POP! POP! POP!

Rivets were popping from the cell's walls, and the prison itself was starting to shudder. The vibration was getting stronger. More rivets came loose and zoomed through the air like bullets.

The ceiling of the cell flew off, revealing open sky. Trees and buildings sped by overhead. The cell was actually inside a truck. A motorcade of SUVs manned by armed guards was escorting the portable prison. No cars were allowed on the road until the convoy had passed.

Magneto didn't care that this highway was off-limits. He stood in the truck's path, his magnetic power pulling it apart. With a sweep of his hand, he sent the SUVs tumbling off the road.

Mystique's guard was watching the scene in horror. With his back pressed up against the bars of her cell, he didn't hear her sneak up behind him. She reached through the bars and twisted his neck. He was dead in seconds.

She took the keychain off his belt and quickly let herself out of her cell.

"This is as far as you go, mutie," a second guard said. He fired his rifle at her, point blank.

Outside, Magneto slowed the battered truck to a halt. He waved his arm, and the metal sides flew off the vehicle. The surviving guard dropped his clipboard and fled for his life.

Pyro picked up the guard's clipboard and started to read the names off the list.

Another prisoner, Jamie Madrox, looked out from what had been his cell.

"I could use a man of your talents," Magneto said to him. Madrox jumped from the truck to the ground, followed by half a dozen exact duplicates of himself. "We all thank you," the aptly named Multiple Man said.

They came upon one cell that was massively secured.

"What do we have here?" asked Magneto.

Pyro read from the clipboard: "Cain Marko. Solitary confinement, zero contact. Prisoner must remain inert at all times. If he builds any momentum, he is virtually unstoppable."

"How fascinating," Magneto replied. He ripped the huge security locks off of the high-tech cage. "What do they call you?" he asked.

"Juggernaut," the mutant responded.

"Mystique is supposed to be here, too," Pyro said.

Magneto stood on a piece of the shattered truck. His magnetic power lifted it—and him—off the ground. He hovered around the truck looking for Mystique.

"Erik?" a voice called out weakly. "Something's wrong."

It was Mystique. She was lying on the ground, curled up in a ball.

She was human now.

The guard had shot her with the cure. Her exotic blue-scaled beauty was a thing of the past. She looked at Magneto with tears in her eyes. "It's still me," she wept. "I still believe in our cause."

Magneto looked at her with disgust.

"I'm sorry but you are no longer one of us. It's such a shame. . . . You were so beautiful."

"Gather the other mutants, Pyro," Magneto continued. "Don't bother with this pathetic human." He looked down at the floor and picked up a strange-looking weapon.

Mystique started to speak, but then stopped. She knew she would have done the same thing in his place. She could only watch sadly as Magneto and the freed mutant prisoners soared off on his magnetically propelled platform.

11

Jean Grey was waking up.

"Jean ...?" a voice asked softly. She was still in the school infirmary.

"Logan?" Jean said.

Wolverine approached her. They stared at one another in silence. The attraction that had always existed between them was even stronger now. They embraced and kissed with furious passion.

Finally, Wolverine broke away. "We have to talk, Jean," he said.

"We can talk later." She smiled.

"No. Now."

"Is he controlling *you*, too?" she asked. "The professor likes to do that. He can read our thoughts, make us do things."

"Jean . . . do you know where Scott is?" Wolverine asked.

"What do you mean?" she replied. The question troubled her. She became confused. "Where am I?"

"What happened to Scott?" Wolverine demanded.

Suddenly, horrifying images came crashing back to her. She started to tremble. "Oh, no!" she shrieked, "I couldn't have . . ."

"Tell me," Wolverine said.

"I killed him," she whispered. "I didn't mean to. But my power . . . was too much for him."

Jean's emotions set off her powers again. Objects rose off surfaces and flew around the room. A lamp crashed into a wall. A telephone whizzed past Wolverine's head. The more Jean tried to control her powers, the less she was able to.

"Kill me," she pleaded, "before I kill someone else."

It was too much for him to process. He didn't know how to respond. After all was said and done, he loved her.

"Please!" she begged. "Kill me!" Her voice no longer sounded human. It had a strange, other-worldly quality. More objects were zooming around the room at dizzying speeds. An oxygen tank crashed into a desk and exploded.

Kill Jean? Wolverine asked himself. *Could I do it? Would her power allow me to?*

"The professor, Jean—he can help you," Wolverine said, trying to calm her down. "He can fix it, make it like it was."

His words had the opposite effect. More objects were flying around the room now. A metal cabinet smashed into a wall. An x-ray machine tore from its moorings and crashed through the ceiling. Energy pulsed off of Jean.

"I don't need to be *fixed*!" she shouted. "I can't go back. I'm *free* now!"

Fighting the waves of energy, Wolverine took

a step toward her. "Jean," he whispered. "Take it easy. Please ... calm down."

She hit him with a huge energy blast, which hurled him into a wall. Wolverine slid down to the floor, unconscious.

Jean raised her hand. The door opened, and she floated through it. No one would keep her trapped. *Especially* not the man who had tried to imprison her mind.

She was through being Charles Xavier's puppet.

12

Beast entered the Oval Office. This time, though, there was no comical animal-like style to his entrance.

He was angry.

"I got your memo," the President said, waving a piece of paper. "You think *resigning* is going to make a difference? That's no way to influence policy."

"Policy is being made without me, Mr. President," Beast replied. "The decision to turn this cure into a weapon was made without me."

"You *knew*?" the President asked.

Beast dropped a file onto the President's desk. Pictures of the "cured" Mystique spilled out of it.

"I know precisely what happened on that convoy," Beast said. "I do have *some* friends in the Pentagon."

"You've got to understand," the President said, "those mutants were a *threat*."

"So you say," Beast replied. "But who decides what is or isn't a threat? Have you even begun to think about what a slippery slope you're on?"

The President nodded soberly. "I have. And I worry. I worry about the amount of power one person can have, I worry about how democracy survives when a man can move cities with his mind."

"As do I," Beast said.

"You understand," the President continued, "that people are scared. They want blood. We were trying to stop something like the prison break from happening."

"It didn't work, did it?" Beast asked.

"No," the President agreed, "and it's only going to get worse."

"All the more reason for me to be where I belong," Beast said. "And that's not *here*." He moved to the door.

"I try to do the right thing, Henry," the President said. "It's not always easy."

"It's not *supposed* to be, sir," he replied as the door closed behind him.

As Storm opened the infirmary door, neither she nor the professor could believe their eyes. The room was in shambles.

Wolverine was just coming to.

"Where is she?" Xavier demanded. "Where is Jean?"

"Gone, Professor," Wolverine said as he struggled to his feet. "And completely out of control."

"She did this?" Storm asked.

Wolverine nodded. "I think she killed Scott," he said softly.

"I warned you about this," Xavier said. "I told you what she was capable of." He closed his eyes to concentrate. "I must find her before she can do more damage."

A few seconds later, the professor opened his

eyes. "It's no use," he said. "She's blocking my mental probes."

"What do we do?" Wolverine asked.

"I think I know where she may have gone," Xavier replied. "I only hope we're not too late."

Elsewhere, Callisto had major news for Magneto. She walked into his underground lair, accompanied by another mutant, a female Omega Mutie. "I've located a powerful mutant," she said.

"Really?" he asked. "How powerful?"

"Massive," she smiled. "Class-five. More powerful than anything I've ever felt."

"Go on," Magneto said, as he leaned back in his chair, pushing away from his desk. He glanced up at Pryo and Juggernaut.

"More powerful," she continued, "than you."

"Then by all means," he said with a smile, "let us find this mutant."

13

The decades had left the tree-lined street largely unchanged. But this time, Charles Xavier and Erik Lensherr came to 1769 Thunderbird Lane separately.

The former friends arrived at virtually the same moment. "She's in the house," Callisto said to Magneto.

Xavier arrived with Wolverine and Storm. "Even with her shields active," the professor said, "I can sense her at this close range."

"How did you know she'd come here?" Wolverine asked.

"Until her powers appeared, this house is where she was happiest," he replied. "She always returned to it in difficult times. I thought she might do so now."

"Is anyone else inside?" Storm asked.

"Just her," Xavier said.

He signaled for Wolverine and Storm to wait outside. Magneto did the same with Callisto and Juggernaut. "No one gets inside," he ordered them.

"You were right, Charles," Magneto said as they approached the house from opposite directions. "This one *is* special." Xavier was trying to probe his former friend's mind, but Magneto wore a special helmet that protected him from mental attack.

Xavier wheeled down the front path next to Magneto, who walked swiftly. "Jean's not well, Erik," he said. "She needs help. You know how much she means to me."

"Yes," Magneto smiled. "But you've no *idea* what she means to *me*."

"She won't go with you," Xavier said. "She's not like the others."

"We'll see, Charles. We'll see." Magneto opened the door, and the two men went inside.

Jean sat in a corner of the living room. "What are you doing here?" she asked.

"I'm here to help you," Xavier said calmly.

"*Help* me, Professor?" she said.

"Your power is too great for you to control," he replied.

"So *you* want to control it?" she asked.

"That's *exactly* his plan," Magneto said.

"That's not true, Jean," Xavier insisted.

"Oh, no?" Magneto asked. "Tell her about your psychic blocks, Charles. Tell her what you *did* to her."

Waves of energy pulsed off Jean's body. The room shook. Objects changed into other forms. Wind swept through the house, though no windows or doors were open.

"Please, Jean," Xavier pleaded. "You need to come home with me."

"I have no home," she whispered. "Not even this place anymore."

Xavier tried to reassure her. "You have a family, Jean, a home. With the X-Men."

"Leave me alone," she said.

"I'm not going anywhere until I can treat you," he said.

Jean moved toward him. "What's wrong with me?" she demanded.

"Nothing!" Magneto said. "Charles, you've always been *afraid* and held her *back*."

"For her own good," Xavier insisted. "She's a danger to herself and others."

"Your way doesn't work, Charles," Magneto said, playing on Jean's anger. "Come with me, Jean. Fight on my side."

Jean wanted to trust Xavier. But he had interfered with her mind and blocked her power. *Was* it for her own good? Or did he have some other agenda?

"Get out!" she screamed. The house shuddered. "Both of you! *Get out!*"

Outside, Wolverine and the others saw the house vibrate. It looked as if an earthquake was taking place on that single lot.

"I'm going in there," he said, popping his claws.

Storm held him back. "The professor told us

to wait here. He said he'd handle this."

"Nice claws," Juggernaut said. "I heard they can cut through anything. Wanna try 'em on me?"

"Don't tempt me, bub," Wolverine responded.

"Look at me, Jean," Xavier pleaded.

"No! Stay out of my head!" she screamed. "My mind belongs to *me*!"

Jean started to glow. More and more energy flowed from her. Objects flew around the room as if in the grip of a hurricane. The blocks Xavier had replaced in her mind were proving to be useless.

Magneto smiled, despite the fact that he, too, was in danger, "Yes, Jean!" he called to her. "Fight him! It's time for you to be *free*!"

"I won't ask again, Jean," Xavier said. "You have forced me to save you from yourself."

Xavier focused all his mutant mental power and launched an attack on Jean's mind.

14

Beads of sweat ran down Xavier's face as he battled Jean on the mental plane. Veins bulged in his forehead and his breathing became labored.

He realized that her mind had become as powerful as he had always feared it would. In a strange way, he was proud of her. But even *she* couldn't control this level of power. Perhaps no one could.

Now it was Xavier's impossible duty to stop her.

For all his efforts, Jean hardly seemed to notice his assault. She remained still, hitting him with mental attacks, even as she dodged or repelled his.

Magneto stood off to the side, pressed against a wall. He magnetically deflected any objects that came near him, but, otherwise, was content to be a spectator to this epic battle.

On the street outside, tensions were running high. Waiting and watching were not the style of any of the mutants there.

Juggernaut, tired of being ignored by Wolverine, butted him from behind, sending him flying. Wolverine landed, rolled, and came up into a crouch, claws gleaming.

"Stop!" Storm shouted as she ran toward them, intent on breaking up the fight.

"Don't worry about them, sister," Callisto said as she tackled Storm. "You've got your own problems."

Storm broke free and kicked at her tattooed foe. But Callisto somehow anticipated the attack, and Storm's feet met only air. She whirled around to strike again, but this time Callisto blocked her assault. It was as if she knew what Storm was going to do before Storm did.

Nearby, Wolverine and Juggernaut raced toward each other and collided with a deafening crash. The impact sent Wolverine flying. Juggernaut kept running, headed to where Wolverine had landed.

Juggernaut viciously fought Wolverine and the pair crashed through an outer wall of the house.

But inside 1769 Thunderbird Lane, reality had been turned upside-down.

Objects were dissolving. Things looked unreal. Gravity no longer ruled, nor did any other rules of physics.

Xavier had used all his mental powers, but they were not enough. He was totally spent. The contest between his power and Jean's was, in the end, no contest at all.

With but a thought, Jean lifted her former mentor from his wheelchair. He hung in the air like a puppet with its strings cut.

"Jean," he pleaded, "don't let it control you."

Xavier's body began to vibrate. His very atoms and molecules were moving at a rate that could not be measured. He felt himself being pulled apart in a million directions. The pain was beyond description.

And then, in a brilliant burst of light, he was gone, atomized into countless particles.

15

Wolverine's mutant senses were on full alert the instant the professor died. Every hair on his body stood up. He looked more animal than human as he jumped off Juggernaut's back.

Callisto and Storm stopped fighting, too. They all sensed that something major had occurred.

Inside the house, everything was suddenly calm. Jean herself was shocked into stillness. She stood in the home in which she had grown up, now help-less and confused as a child.

Magneto approached her carefully. "Do you know what you've done?" he asked gently.

"You've freed me," he said. "You've freed *yourself*. Xavier wanted us all to follow his failed path of compromise with humans. He refused to see things as they really are."

Jean seemed to be listening to him. "Join me," he continued, "and you will be free from this day forward." Magneto extended his hand to Jean. She hesitated. He looked at her, and his eyes seemed to peer into her very soul.

She took his hand.

When Magneto and Jean appeared in the doorway, Wolverine sped over to them. "What happened, Jean?" he demanded. "Where's the professor?"

Jean kept on walking as if he wasn't even there. Juggernaut and Callisto joined her and Magneto, and the quartet left the scene.

Wolverine and Storm ran to the house. Inside, they saw the professor's empty wheelchair.

Storm's eyes clouded over and so did the skies outside.

Wolverine's wail of sorrow carried across the silver-gray skies.

The sky was still gray the next day, but this time it was not Storm's doing. Rain poured down on the cemetery where the school's students, teachers, and friends had gathered.

There were two graves, though there were no remains that could be buried in either one of them. Each had a simple headstone.

Storm looked around. There was no sign of Wolverine. Was he holed up somewhere, trying to make sense of all that had happened? Or worse, was he out taking some kind of action that he— and the X-Men—might live to regret?

It was raining too hard to wait any longer. Storm stood to speak. She didn't know what she was going to say until the words came out of her mouth.

"We live in an age of darkness," she began. "A world of fear and anger, hate and intolerance."

Emotion choked her for a second. As she took a sip of water, she glanced up and saw Rogue. The girl looked devastated. Bobby stood next to her, his arm around her raincoat-draped shoulder.

"For most, this is the way things are and always will be," Storm continued. "But in every age there are those who fight against it."

Storm looked up and saw Kitty and Colossus. Kitty nodded, as if to tell her she was saying the things they were all feeling.

Storm continued, "There was Moses, who led his people out of slavery but never saw the promised land himself. There was Abraham Lincoln, who freed the slaves but never lived to see his country at peace. And there was Martin Luther King Jr. who fought for equal rights but was struck down by an assassin's bullet."

Storm saw that the newer students were listening intently, hanging on her every word. She realized that what she was saying had to be more than just a tribute to the past. It had to be about the future, too.

"It wasn't something they asked to do," Storm said. "They were chosen. And he was chosen, too." She gestured toward the professor's headstone.

"Charles Xavier was born into a world he tried to heal. It was a mission he never saw accomplished."

Storm then looked at Cyclops' grave. "Scott Summers was the one that Professor Xavier chose to lead the X-Men," she said. "Scott did so without fear or hesitation. But Scott, too, will not be with us when Professor Xavier's dream becomes reality.

"Xavier's teachings live on with us, his students," Storm concluded. "Wherever we may go, we must carry on his vision. The vision of a world united."

Storm walked back to her chair and sat down. She had spoken bravely and from the heart.

But terrible facts were staring her in the face. Her mentor and her teammate were dead. Magneto was about to launch an offensive, and Jean was with him. The government had a mutant cure they were using as a weapon. And when she needed Wolverine the most, he was nowhere to be found.

Everything was falling apart—and it was all falling on her.

16

It wasn't uncommon to hear sobbing around the mansion these days. But it was rare to hear it, as Iceman did, from Kitty Pryde's room.

He knocked on the door. "Come in," Kitty said.

Nervously, he entered the room. Kitty was really nice and really cute. But Rogue was his girlfriend. Kitty was his friend. His teammate. That's all.

"It's okay, Kitty," he said. "We're all upset."

She cried even harder. "You have Rogue, Bobby. I'm all alone here. I miss home, winter, snow."

"Uh, I don't know if you noticed," he said. "We

get plenty of snow here in Westchester."

"It's not the same," she said. "We're at this weird school for weird kids. Don't you miss normal life?"

"What's normal?" he asked.

"I wish I knew," she replied. She was smiling a small smile. Iceman was glad that he was cheering her up a little.

He saw her ice skates sitting in the bottom of her closet. "Hey—I've got an idea," he said. He picked them up and handed them to her.

"Bobby," she said. "It's way too warm out to skate on the pond. And the rink in White Plains is closed for repairs."

"In case you forgot, Ms. Pryde, my code name is *Iceman*," he said.

A minute later, they were on the edge of the small pond next to the mansion. Iceman knelt down and put a hand on the water's surface. Ice crystals started to gather around his hand. Then the chilling effect spread out, and in a few seconds, the entire surface of the pond was a solid sheet of ice.

"Madame," he said, motioning her to the ice. Kitty laced up her skates, then took a small step onto the frozen pond.

"How far down does this go?" she asked.

"It's solid all the way through," said Iceman. "I think I might even have messed up the mansion's plumbing."

Kitty held out her hand. "If you're so sure about it, why not join me?"

"No skates," he said. "But on the other hand … or foot …"

He reached down and touched his hand to his sneakers, forming a blade that turned his sneakers into ice skates. He stepped onto the ice, slid over to Kitty, and took her hand. They moved gracefully around the frozen surface.

"See?" he said. "This place can be home, too."

After a while, she skated them to a halt. "Thank you, Bobby," she said, kissing him on the cheek.

Unnoticed by either of them, Rogue had been watching from the mansion. Tears flowing down her cheeks, she turned away from her window.

Outside, Iceman just stared at Kitty. He liked

skating with her, holding hands with her, and of course, being kissed by her. But then he thought about Rogue and their argument. He slid away from his skating partner.

Kitty frowned. "We should get back inside," she said, and skated to the shore.

Storm found Wolverine in the professor's office. The lights were off.

"You should have come to the funeral," she said.

"I don't do funerals," Wolverine replied. "Been to too many."

"I'm just glad you didn't go off on some half-baked quest," she said.

"Actually," he said, "I've been thinking I should go after Jean; to try to help her."

"Why can't you let her go, Logan?" Storm demanded. "Why can't you see the truth? She's gone over to Magneto's side. End of story."

Wolverine didn't respond.

"You love her, Logan," Storm continued. "But she made her choice. It's time to make ours. I've lost Scott and Jean, my two oldest friends. And

I've lost the professor—the closest thing to a father I've ever had. You try to *save* her—and you could end up dead, too. She's beyond our help. Whatever happened to her at the lake changed her forever."

Storm left the room. She knew Wolverine would do what he felt he had to do.

Mutants from across the world gathered at the Brotherhood campsite, hidden deep in the woods. They had heard Magneto's call, and came to join him.

"This is Jean Grey," Magneto announced to the group. There were gasps from a few mutants. Others booed. Magneto raised his hand in a request for silence.

"Jean has started on the journey to our point of view," he said. "Please make her feel welcome."

Magneto pointed at a small scrap of metal on the ground. It rose up and floated to Jean. "What's this for?" she asked.

"An experiment," he replied. "Tell me—what do you see when you look at that?"

She stared at the jagged fragment. "I see ... the atoms it's made of," she said. "Actually . . . I *feel* them."

"Tell me that kind of power isn't wonderful, Jean," he said. "Tell me that it doesn't feel good to be free of all restraints."

"A person shouldn't have this much power," she said.

"Is that *you* speaking?" he asked. "Or Charles? He was wrong, Jean."

"What do you *want* from me?" she pleaded.

"What I want for everyone here," Magneto said. "I want you to be what you are, as nature intended."

Jean walked away from him and disappeared into the woods, but she didn't leave the campsite. Magneto was sure it was only a matter of time before she would begin to see things his way.

17

It felt strange for Storm to be sitting at Professor X's desk. But it also felt right. She was glad she had decided to hold the meeting here. Seated around the room were Rogue, Iceman, Colossus, Kitty, and Beast.

Notably missing, once again, was Wolverine.

"You were here at the beginning, Dr. McCoy," Storm said. "What do you think the X-Men should do now?"

"To begin with," Beast said, "I think you should call me Hank. Or Beast. Dr. McCoy's too stuffy for a guy covered in blue fur."

"Okay, then. What do you think we should do, uh, Hank?"

"I think—no, I *know*—that we have to keep things going here," he said. "The professor never said it would be easy to make his dream come true. But we all know it's a dream *worth* keeping alive."

"Noble words," Colossus said. "But are we not just targets here? Maybe we need to go into hiding. Stealth works for Magneto."

"Is he our new role model?" Kitty asked. "Working in secret isn't the way to win people's trust. We have to be visible so any mutant who needs support can find us."

A wildly ringing doorbell interrupted the debate. The group ran to the mansion's front entrance. Storm opened the door to find a young man in a raincoat standing there.

"I hear this is a safe place for mutants," the newcomer said. "My name is Warren Worthington."

"As in . . . the inventor of the cure nobody asked for?" Iceman asked.

"Actually, that would be my father," Warren replied. "And I'm the one he mainly wanted to, um, cure."

Warren took off his coat, and his wings spread to their full span. The X-Men were silent for a second. It was an awesome sight, even to them.

"Well, Warren," Iceman said. "Once upon a time, this *was* a safe place. But not anymore."

Storm gently but firmly pushed Iceman aside. "Mr. Drake is young, Warren. He doesn't see the big picture yet. We can provide what you're looking for."

"Thank you," Warren said, relieved. "And you are . . . ?"

"I am Ororo Munroe, also known as Storm," she replied. "And if no one has any objections . . . I believe I am the acting director of the School for Gifted Youngsters." She looked at Beast, who, given his long history with the school, was the only one present who might challenge her.

"Seems like the best choice to me," he said.

"Thank you, Hank," Storm said. "Now, Iceman, please find Mr. Worthington a room. The rest of us will go tell the students the news. Everyone needs to know that the school is still open for business."

Iceman opened a door and switched the light on. "This one isn't too bad," he said to Warren Worthington. "Probably not as spiffy as what you're used to, though. The dorms aren't the best kept-up part of the mansion."

"It's not *anything* like what I'm used to," Warren smiled. "That's what I like about it."

"Glad to hear it," Iceman said. "If you're hungry, the kitchen's down the hall."

"Right now I just want to sleep for a week," Warren said.

"Sounds like a plan to me," Iceman said.

As he walked back down the hall, Iceman was hopeful. He had a good feeling about Storm taking over. Having Beast around felt right, too. And now the son of the guy who created the cure was joining up with them.

He wanted to set things straight with Rogue. He loved her; he would stick with her. Sure, Kitty was pretty and nice. But Rogue needed him and he would be there for her. He'd tell her so right now.

There was no response when he knocked on her door. He opened it a crack. "Rogue?" he called quietly. "You awake?" Still no answer.

He opened the door, only to find that there was no one inside. Iceman saw a newspaper on Rogue's bed. It was opened to an article with the headline MUTANT CURE CLINIC OPENS IN WESTCHESTER.

"You picked a heck of a time to check out, Charlie. You, too, Summers."

Wolverine stood before Professor Xavier and Cyclops' graves. "So, guys, what do we do now?" he asked. "Maybe we should all just take the cure. Presto—no more 'mutant problem.' 'Course, guys like Magneto are never gonna do that. Guess that means we can't, either, huh?"

Wolverine felt a little foolish talking to the air like this. He was half-expecting the professor to answer him. He remembered all the times he'd been in the middle of doing something and gotten a sudden mental summons from Xavier. He couldn't believe he'd never get another.

Suddenly, he *did* sense a mind calling to his. "Come to me, Logan. Help me. Please."

Jean.

"Where are you, Jeanie?" he whispered. The answer came to him in a jolting series of images.

Wolverine jumped on his motorbike and sped off.

18

Magneto's guards never knew what hit them. Wolverine silently took them out and made sure they hit the ground softly.

He heard voices up ahead. He recognized Magneto's, but there were many others he didn't know. As he made his way forward, Wolverine saw the glow of campfires, around which were dozens of mutants, perhaps as many as a hundred. This was big. Even Magneto had never gathered so many mutants together before. It was an army.

Magneto stood in the center of the crowd, and Jean stood nearby. "They say we're criminals," he said. "They wish to *cure* us. They have their weapons.

We have ours. Soon we will strike at the source of the cure and wipe it from the face of the Earth."

Wolverine slowly made his way toward Jean and Magneto. He wasn't sure what he would do when he got there. His instincts generally told him the right thing to do. He hoped they would now.

Suddenly, a burning log flared. It lit up his face enough for Jean to see him. "Logan," she called out. Her features softened. She was, once again, the Jean he knew.

"I'm here, Jeannie," he said. "Here to get you away from this creep."

"I do admire your persistence." Magneto smiled. "But the lady has chosen sides. I won't allow you to contain her again."

"You won't *allow*? Do you think you're gonna scare me off?" Wolverine asked through gritted teeth. He now stood inches from Magneto.

Magneto put his palm on Wolverine's chest, and a magnetic pulse shot from the hand, which sent Wolverine flying. His Adamantium-laced body arced over the forest, finally landing hard in a thicket of trees.

Magneto's power had done more than just propel Wolverine away. It had damaged his internal organs. Bleeding, more dead than alive, Wolverine dragged himself through the brush. It seemed like Magneto hadn't sent anyone after him, and he wasn't going to wait around for him to think of it. Ignoring his pain as best he could, Wolverine headed back to the school.

Cure clinics were sprouting up all over the place. Maybe it was someone's idea of a joke to put this one so close to the School for Gifted Youngsters.

Iceman knew the address from the article, but he wouldn't have had any trouble finding the place even if he didn't. There was a crowd of shouting protestors whose anger was directed at the long line of mutants who had come to be "cured."

Iceman ran the length of the line. Maybe Rogue had come there. It was all his fault. He should have realized she wasn't just jealous over his feelings for Kitty. She was jealous of *anybody* who could touch another person. A chance to be "normal" would be *exactly* what she would go for. And who could blame her?

He was approaching the end of the line, and

there was still no sign of Rogue. But he did see someone he recognized.

"Pyro!" Iceman exclaimed.

"What a small world!" the fire-controlling mutant said. "What are you doing here? Betraying your fellow X-muties and their stupid dream?"

"I'm looking for Rogue," Iceman replied.

"Ah, young love," Pyro chuckled. "But you're missing the big picture, pal."

"Spare me Magneto One-oh-One," Iceman said. "I don't have any time to waste."

"Neither do I." Pyro laughed. He clicked a cigarette lighter on with his thumb. As he concentrated, the small flame grew larger. At his mental command, it grew to the size of a boulder.

Then, with a wave of his arm, he tossed the fireball in the direction of the clinic. The wood-frame building caught fire almost immediately.

Iceman started to run toward it, but a sudden explosion knocked him off his feet. As he stood up, he saw Pyro disappear into the night.

People were streaming out of the clinic. Protestors were fleeing, too. An elderly woman had fallen and a young boy was trying to help her up. A flaming wall was about to fall on top of them.

Suddenly, a wall of ice appeared and shielded them. As the flames melted the ice, Iceman kept adding to the shield he had created. The old woman and the boy were grabbed by a couple of people and taken to safety.

When everyone was safely away from the building Iceman let the shield go. The clinic was now a flaming pile of rubble. Fire engines were approaching, too late to do any good.

And he hadn't found Rogue.

Similar attacks took place at cure clinics around the country. If there was any doubt about who was behind the attacks, it was soon made clear by a video sent to television stations.

Magneto's message was short and to the point.

"Humans created this cure," he said on the video. "Humans must destroy it. If you do not . . . then *I will*. So long as the cure exists, our war will rage. Your cities will not be safe."

He paused for emphasis, then pointed directly into the camera.

"*You* will not be safe."

19

The assault unit was armed to the teeth. They were prepared to face a hundred or more mutant fanatics at the campsite—possibly even Magneto himself. They'd been given the location by an inside source: Mystique.

Having been betrayed by Magneto, she returned the favor by giving the government the location of Magneto's base of operations. Now the military had come to the location where she'd told them he'd be.

The unit leader was wary but confident. "Satellite and thermal imagery say there are upwards of one hundred muties here," he said to his lieutenant. "But we have enough men, hardware, and cure-bullets to handle anything." He sounded as if he was trying to convince himself.

"Surrender now," the commander said over a booming sound system. "Otherwise, you will lose your powers and quite possibly your lives."

The soldiers started moving forward. Army helicopters appeared in the sky, lighting up the area as if it was New Year's Eve.

But what they saw was not at all what they had expected.

The mutants all looked exactly the same. Not just their clothes. They were all the same height and build. Each one even had the same exact *face* as all of the others.

As the troops approached, the mutants suddenly united into a single man. He smiled and raised his arms in surrender. "Okay, I give up," James Madrox said. He had just demonstrated his mutant power. He could make many exact copies of himself.

As Magneto had planned, Multiple Man was the perfect decoy to divert the government's resources.

Henry McCoy's voice boomed through the speaker-phone from the Oval Office. "I have reason to believe," he said, "that Magneto has left his campsite. His most likely target is Worthington Labs."

"We're aware of that," Senator Trask said.

"May I suggest . . ." Hank began.

"You may *not*," Trask barked. "You walked away from having a say in any of this." He ended the call.

"It's starting, sir," Trask said to the President.

"We'll deal with whatever Magneto throws at us," the President said. "I will do everything in my power to get the cure to every mutant who wants it. I will not allow a terrorist like Magneto to steal their right to decide."

Wolverine's healing power had repaired the damage Magneto had done to him. He was ready to go after the Brotherhood again.

Now, as he approached the *X-Jet* hangar, he hoped Storm was already there. He wanted to get into the air as soon as possible. They needed to get to Alcatraz so they'd have a chance to stop Magneto and save Jean before it was too late. He didn't know how they would accomplish all of that, but was certain they'd figure out a way.

Wolverine opened the hangar door. As he had hoped, Storm was waiting there. But she wasn't alone.

Iceman was there. So were Kitty, Colossus, and Beast. Warren Worthington III was with the group, too.

"What's all this about?" Wolverine asked, although he knew the answer. And he knew he didn't like it.

"We're coming with you," Iceman said.

"We're ready," Colossus said. "We trained for this."

"This is all our fight," Storm said, "not just yours."

Wolverine shook his head. Their hearts were in the right place. But, aside from Storm, they weren't as ready as they wanted to think they were.

"This isn't going to be like in class or the Danger Room," he said. "It's going to be a real battle. We get on that plane and we're not students and teachers anymore. We're soldiers."

"We're X-Men," Iceman said proudly. "All of us."

One by one, Wolverine looked each of them in the eye. They were serious. They really wanted to do this. And he really needed their help.

He motioned toward the plane. "Get in. Let's go!"

The crew climbed into the jet. Wolverine followed behind them, but then hesitated for a second. He sensed a figure in the shadows.

"You almost missed the flight, Rogue," he said. "Let's go."

Rogue emerged from the darkness. "I'm not going," she said.

Wolverine saw immediately that her gloves were off.

"You did it, didn't you?" he asked. "You took the cure."

"You don't know what it's like," she said, "to be afraid of your powers. To be afraid to get close to anyone. To know you can never go home again."

"Actually, kid," Wolverine said, "I do know what it's like. And I'm not going to judge you. I just hope," he added, "that you didn't do this for Drake."

"I did it for me," she said.

"Then you did the right thing," Wolverine replied. He boarded the jet.

"Be careful," Rogue whispered. The door shut behind him with a clang that echoed through the hangar. Then the jet's engines started with a deafening roar.

Within seconds, they were airborne.

⋇⋇⋇

Golden Gate Park stretches through the middle of San Francisco, ending at San Francisco Bay, across from which lies Alcatraz. Parts of the park are as tree-filled as any forest.

It was among those trees that the mutant army was now hiding.

"I sense him," Callisto said to Magneto. "Leech is in the southeast corner, third level of the lab."

"Then it's time to make our move," Magneto said. "Next stop: Alcatraz."

As he took the lead, followed closely by Callisto, Juggernaut, and Pyro, Magneto looked back at Jean. He could see she was still not sure about all this. Even so, she hadn't left his group. He motioned for the others to go ahead and he stopped to speak to her.

"That cure is meant for all of us, Jean," he said. "You may choose not to go down my path in the future. But this cure means mutants will have no choice about their futures at all."

"Let's go," was all she said.

As Jean fell in with the rest of Magneto's followers, her mind was racing. Was she doing the right thing? It was all so clear to Magneto. Professor Xavier, too, had been sure of *his* mission. Why was it so hard for *her* to know the right thing to do?

She had all this power. What was she supposed to do with it?

Things were tense onboard the *X-Jet*. For many of them, this was their first real mission. It was one thing to survive in the Danger Room. Despite its name, it was actually quite safe—a great place to train. But today was different.

Storm was piloting the jet. Wolverine sat beside her. "If she's there," Storm began. "If she's sided with Magneto . . ."

"If she's there," he replied, looking straight ahead, "I want you to get everyone away from her."

"What are you going to do?" Storm asked.

"I know what she's capable of," he said. "If I have to . . . I'll choose the lesser evil."

Storm shivered. She feared for her friends.

20

San Francisco is no stranger to earthquakes. They are a fact of life for those who live there. The 1906 quake was just the most famous and most destructive.

So when the Golden Gate Bridge began to shake and rattle, people thought it was another earthquake. The bridge vibrated so hard it actually began to pull apart.

Cars and trucks rolled in all directions. The sounds of screeching brakes and crashing vehicles filled the air, followed by desperate screams and pleas for help.

But this was no natural disaster. It was manmade.

More specifically, it was *mutant* made.

Magneto was standing on the Golden Gate Bridge, directing his magnetic energy at the structure beneath his feet. Only a small vein bulging on his forehead gave any hint this might be a strain on him. He rode the bridge as if it was his own personal amusement park ride.

Then, as the mutant army on the shore and the government soldiers on Alcatraz watched in awe, the bridge, which connected San Francisco with Marin County to the north, changed direction! It turned and twisted as if it was made of rubber.

Magneto was transforming it into a connection between San Francisco and Alcatraz. Under his command, the majestic ribbon of steel swung through the sky.

The approaching *X-Jet* was right in its path. Using all her skills as a pilot, Storm narrowly avoided a collision with the wildly moving bridge.

"You don't need a mutant guidebook to know who's responsible for *that*," Wolverine said.

The younger mutants on the plane were stunned by this display of power. "One man did that?" Iceman whispered.

"And he's not as powerful as Jean," Wolverine replied. "That's what you signed on for, kids."

Wolverine's comment was met with silence as the young mutants continued to stare out the jet's windows with mouths agape.

Magneto led his followers across the bridge. They were deaf to the screams of the injured and dying in the wrecked cars and trucks.

Jean Grey marched a few yards behind Magneto, her senses absorbing the suffering all around her. She heard the agonized thoughts of the victims as if they were screaming in her ears.

A little girl was trapped along with her family in a silver Mercedes SUV. She looked to Jean, who thought the girl looked so much like herself as a child. They had the same nose, the same eyes, the same color hair.

Jean could hear the fear and sadness in the girl's mind. It reminded her of what she, herself, once was: a little girl with a good heart. The girl's thoughts—indeed, the thoughts of all the humans trapped on the bridge—were starting to overwhelm Jean.

"Stay strong, Jean," Magneto said to her.

Jean shook her head. She was unsure what she should do.

"Come with us," Magneto said.

"Don't tell me what to do," she replied, anger creeping into her voice.

"I'm not telling you what to do," he said. "I'm asking for your help. Help us destroy the only thing that can control you."

"*You're* trying to control me," she hissed. "Just like he did."

Magneto slowly backed away from Jean. He looked back and made eye contact with the mother of the little girl in the car. The mother quickly moved to lock the doors of her SUV. Magneto grinned as he turned and resumed the march. He would deal with whatever Jean ultimately decided.

So would the rest of the world.

With Magneto at its head, the mutant army broke into a running charge. They came off the bridge and onto Alcatraz. Juggernaut put his head down and raced forward at top speed.

But, while his legs were moving, he stayed in one place, floating a few inches above the ground.

"Hold back," Magneto commanded. He was the one keeping Juggernaut from joining the battle. "I have a special job for you."

As the other mutants charged forward, the U.S. military advanced toward them. The soldiers carried what looked like standard missile launchers.

Magneto laughed and dispatched a magnetic assault on the launchers. But his power had no effect.

The launchers were made of plastic.

The soldiers fired football-shaped plastic cylinders from their launchers. The cylinders sailed through the air—then exploded into clouds of vapor.

Small shards came flying from the clouds, shooting out in all directions, hitting everything in sight. Despite this, no one seemed harmed. But as the mutants charged forward again, they realized the truth.

The shards contained the *cure*. The mutant powers of anyone hit by them were gone.

Guessing that this would be the military's strategy, Magneto had held his key allies back. He, Juggernaut, Avalanche, Callisto, and Pyro all still had their powers.

Then, with a series of flaming bolts, Pyro melted the remaining weapons into puddles of plastic goo.

Magneto turned to Juggernaut. "As I said, I have a mission for you," he said. "Everything depends on your success."

"Just tell me what to do," Juggernaut replied eagerly.

"Listen carefully," Magneto said. "Southeast corner. Third level. Get the boy. Alive or dead. Just get him."

"Alive or dead. Got it," Juggernaut said, smiling broadly.

With his head down, Juggernaut ran forward. "Nothing can stop the Juggernaut!" he shouted. It didn't seem like anything would.

Still standing amid the carnage on the bridge, Jean Grey saw a familiar sight in the sky.

The *X-Jet* was descending on Alcatraz.

Jean watched as the plane landed on a corner of the island. She saw the X-Men emerge from it. There was a time when she would have been right there with them. She took a step forward, as if she thought she might be able to join them again.

Then she remembered what she had done; remembered what she could never undo.

She stopped in her tracks.

21

"**O**ne more step, and you're dead, muties," the squad leader said.

He and his men stood between the X-Men and the main lab building.

"Wait!" Warren Worthington III shouted. "Let me explain."

"There's nothing to explain, freak," the soldier snapped at him. "Our orders are to stop the mutants. That means you."

"Stop! Don't fire!" a desperate voice called. It was Warren's father. The soldiers weren't sure what to do now. He wasn't their commander, but it was his lab they were supposed to be protecting.

"What are you doing here?" Warren Worthington Sr. asked his son.

"Helping you, Dad," he said.

Storm stepped forward. "Magneto is going after the source of the cure," she said. "Where is it?"

The older Worthington hesitated for a moment.

"I can't just turn it over. My son needs my help," he said, on the verge of tears.

"Dad, please," Warren said. "You have to trust the X-Men." He paused. "I do."

"The cure is stockpiled under the building," his father said. "But ..."

"But what?" Wolverine said. "Tell us *exactly* where it is."

"The cure means nothing," Worthington Sr. said. "It's the *source* Magneto wants."

"What do you mean 'the source'?" Wolverine demanded.

Worthington Sr. continued, "A mutant. A little boy. We create it from his DNA."

Anger and disgust welled up inside Wolverine. It was all he could do to keep from running his claws through this man.

"Where is he?" Wolverine demanded. "Tell us."

His claws popped out. "Tell us *now*."

"Dad … please," Warren begged.

"Southeast corner, third level," Worthington said.

Wolverine led the X-Men past the soldiers. The commander signaled his men to let them go through.

"Good call, bub," Wolverine said. "You might just live through this."

Even though they were without their cure launchers, the soldiers by the building still hugely outnumbered Magneto and his inner circle. The troops cautiously advanced on the mutants.

"Are you ready?" Magneto asked Pyro.

Nervous but eager to please, Pyro nodded. He had never attempted anything as big as this.

Facing the redirected bridge, Pyro focused on one specific stack of wrecked, smoking cars. He concentrated, turning the flame that licked around the edges of the pile into a huge ball of fire. None of the soldiers had yet noticed what he was doing.

Wolverine had.

"Take cover!" he called to the soldiers. He and the other X-Men were racing toward them.

"Too late, Wolverine," Magneto said.

The stack of burning cars—propelled by his magnetic power—was hurtling right at them. Flaming gas tanks, exploding in midair, rained burning fuel down on the island.

A second later, the fireball smashed into the midst of the fleeing soldiers and cured mutants.

Taking advantage of the confusion, Magneto and his crew raced toward the main building. They easily plowed through any remaining soldiers. The X-Men ran to intercept them.

Juggernaut was almost at the front door when suddenly, Colossus jumped in front of him, leading with a metallic fist that seemed as if it could stop anything.

But it couldn't stop Juggernaut. He slammed forward, knocking into Colossus, who went flying backward.

Juggernaut hadn't even slowed down. He crashed through a brick wall.

Wolverine started to run after him, but Magneto sent a group of mutants to stop him. Wolverine couldn't chase the single-minded Juggernaut now.

"Kitty!" Wolverine called out. "Protect the kid! We can't let Juggernaut get him!"

"On it," she called, and raced into the building. If Leech was where Worthington Sr. said he was, she'd have no problem finding him. Getting past Juggernaut would be another thing.

Nearby, thunder boomed out of the cloud-filled skies as Storm fired lightning at Magneto. She was determined to keep him from getting any closer to the Worthington Labs building. But his magnetic energy was keeping her bolts of electricity from hurting him.

A short distance away, Henry McCoy was proving he wasn't just a politician. He launched into Magneto's forces with a vicious, brutal assault worthy of someone code-named Beast.

" 'Scuse me, pardon me, 'scuse me," he shouted, leaping from one foe to the next, kicking, punching, and head-butting them.

Not far from Beast, Warren Worthington III, looking like an angry angel, flew into the battle. Again and again, he hit Magneto's forces from above. They never knew where or when he'd strike next.

This enraged Magneto. It was bad enough the youth's father was an enemy to mutants. Now the son was also proving to be one. The master of magnetism levitated a large piece of metal, then sent it shooting through the air. It hit young Warren hard, knocking him out of the sky. The winged mutant made a painful landing.

Before he could even get to his feet, Pyro was on him, a ball of fire dancing between his hands. "No big daddy to save you now." He laughed. "Hope you don't mind the smell of burning feathers."

Suddenly Pyro's hands were covered in ice! The fireball sizzled as it melted the frigid coating to steam. But the flame soon went out completely.

"You and I have some unfinished business, Pyro," Iceman said. He had to keep Pyro's attention off the injured Worthington.

"Sure do," Pyro said. "Fire versus Ice. Sounds like a wrestling bill."

"Bring it on," Iceman said. He launched a huge ice bolt at Pyro, who responded with a rolling wave of flame.

Nearby, Storm distracted some of Magneto's forces with wind-driven rain. Then Wolverine and Beast plowed through them as if they were bowling pins.

All over the island, the X-Men were holding their own against Magneto's forces. As Wolverine had warned the new team members, this wasn't a Danger Room session. But the lessons they learned in the Danger Room were what made them so good today. They fought like a team.

It felt like the realization of Professor Xavier's dream. Wolverine was proud of these new X-Men. They had been tested and they had come through.

But their real trial by fire was just beginning.

22

Inside the Worthington Labs building, Kitty heard a muffled explosion. A second later, there was a louder one.

Then the wall in front of her shattered into millions of pieces of plaster and concrete.

Juggernaut had arrived.

When he saw the slender young woman blocking his path, he exploded with laughter. No way was she stopping him! Juggernaut raced forward and grabbed her.

But as he did, Kitty touched his arm. Her phasing power made him lose his solid form, and he sank into the floor. When Juggernaut had collapsed up to his neck, she let go of him. He instantly became solid again, but now he was stuck in the floor. Passing through a wall, Kitty took off for Leech's room.

Juggernaut was angry. He tensed his muscles and, with a savage roar, ripped himself free.

Kitty heard the sounds of walls and doors being smashed behind her. One thing was for certain: Juggernaut wasn't going to be able to sneak up on her.

Kitty made it to a hallway on the third level. *This should be it*, she thought. From the silence around her, it seemed as if she had given Juggernaut the slip.

She passed through the wall and found herself in a room filled with children's toys and posters.

"Please don't hurt me," a voice pleaded. She looked around but didn't see anyone.

Then she saw Leech hiding behind the bed. He was shivering with fear. "I'm not going to hurt you," Kitty said. "I've come to get you out of here."

The boy looked at her, his eyes full of hope. He wanted to believe her, but he wasn't sure whom he could trust anymore.

"Promise?" he said.

"Promise."

Kitty reached her hand out. Leech hesitated, but finally took it. Together, they walked to the far wall. "Don't be afraid," she said. "I can walk *both* of us through it." But when she tried to do it, nothing happened.

"Your powers won't work with me," Leech said.

"Well, there's always the old-school method," Kitty said as she walked to the door. But before she could reach it, Juggernaut burst through a wall. The huge mutant towered over Kitty and Leech. He looked at them, enjoying the moment. Then he lowered his head to charge.

Kitty stood there as if she was admitting there was no escape.

But at the last instant before impact, she let her knees buckle under her. She pushed Leech to the side and she dropped to the ground like a sack of potatoes.

With all his strength, Juggernaut smashed into the wall where Kitty had been standing an instant before. There was a loud cracking sound as his head hit the wall, but the wall was undamaged.

Leech had switched off Juggernaut's mutant power, too.

Juggernaut bounced off the wall. He staggered back, his legs wobbly. He was still much bigger and stronger than Kitty and Leech. He could easily take them both. All he needed was a couple of seconds to recover from his impact with the wall.

He wasn't going to get those seconds.

Colossus came racing through the hole in the wall that Juggernaut had created when he'd arrived. Although Colossus' powers were also turned off by Leech, he was plenty strong even without them. He reared back and punched Juggernaut hard. Juggernaut collapsed to the floor, unconscious.

Colossus helped Kitty and Leech to their feet.

"You really came to save me?" the boy asked.

"We really did," Kitty replied. The three of them walked out of the room. The X-Men had Leech. Now all they had to do was keep him—and themselves—from getting killed.

23

Outside the lab building, the battle raged on.

Pyro had Iceman surrounded with a wall of flame that kept inching closer. Iceman poured all his energy into an ice barrier, but it was melting as fast as he could build it.

Iceman knew he couldn't last much longer. There was a stunt he'd only tried out in the Danger Room. It might save him today—if he could pull it off!

"Nothing to lose," he said as he closed his eyes to focus his concentration. He took a deep breath.

Iceman opened his eyes and snapped into action. He constructed an ice ramp that soared up over the fire wall. Then he turned and shot a shaft of ice at the ground behind him. The recoil shot him up the slide, and he kept adding to the slide in front of him as he went. The part of the slide that was behind him melted as soon as he was over the wall.

Now for the *hard* part.

With Pyro shooting bolts of flame at him, Iceman created a roller coaster of ice slides. As he slid up and down the ramps, he gained more and more speed.

Pyro was melting the slides, but Iceman was varying the pattern of the ramps he was building. Pyro couldn't predict where they would lead. Iceman gained more and more speed, finally making an extremely sharp turn and coming around swiftly *behind* Pyro.

"Fight fair, you human Popsicle," Pyro shouted.

"Riiiight." Iceman laughed. He was enjoying this.

Forming a log of solid ice and holding it in his arms like a battering ram, Iceman zoomed right into Pyro just as the fire-mutant was turning to meet the attack. Too late. The log shattered as it hit Pyro, and he went down like a ton of bricks.

Iceman stood over him, ready for anything. But Pyro didn't move.

"Guess he's *out cold*," Iceman said aloud. He thought Rogue would have found that funny.

Callisto was proving to be more of a challenge than Storm had expected.

The tattooed young woman's mutant power enabled her to anticipate Storm's winds and even her lightning attacks. No matter what strategy Storm tried on her, Callisto was able to evade it.

The more Storm concentrated and focused, the easier it seemed for Callisto to dodge her assaults.

I'm thinking too much, Storm realized. As a youngster, she had had to fend for herself in dangerous situations, relying more on instinct than thought. It was time to call on those skills again.

Storm relaxed her control over the elements. She stood a few feet away from Callisto and gestured for her to come closer.

Overconfident, Callisto obliged and landed the first few blows. She was an expert at martial arts, and that, combined with her mutant powers, made her nearly unbeatable.

Storm went into non-thinking mode, acting and reacting on instinct alone. Callisto was unable to predict Storm's blows, and therefore unable to defend herself against them. Storm knew it was only a matter of time before Callisto was able to figure out her fighting patterns. She would have to finish up fast.

With a series of moves that she would never have been able to repeat, Storm did just that. She hit Callisto low, high, and in between. She attacked and never stopped.

And when it was all over, Callisto lay helpless, begging for mercy.

But while the X-Men were having small successes, Magneto was still on the offensive. He was determined to destroy the lab complex. Whether or not he gained control of Leech, he would not let Worthington's building stand.

Glowing with magnetic energy, he rose high above the battleground. "This cursed place will exist no more," he shouted. Waves of energy glowed more and more intensely around him, shattering chunks of brick and concrete off the building.

Wolverine shook away the mutants who were pulling at him. He was too far from Magneto to do anything to stop him. But, somehow, he had to stop him. Destroying the cure was one thing, but there were still people in the building and every one of them would be killed.

"Wolverine!" a voice called out. "We saved the boy. Kitty has taken him to safety." It was Colossus, in full-metal mode, emerging from the building.

"Good work, tin man," Wolverine said, then gestured toward Magneto. "How's your pitching arm?"

"Never better, comrade," Colossus replied.

"Then it's fastball-special time, bub!"

Colossus nodded in agreement. He picked Wolverine up and reared back, then stepped forward and unleashed him in a perfect throw.

Magneto didn't see the mutant missile hurtling toward him until it was too late. Wolverine slammed into him, and the two of them hit the ground. Scrambling to his feet, Wolverine grabbed Magneto by the collar. "Where is she?" he demanded. *Where is Jean?*

Magneto laughed and hurled Wolverine away from him with a blast of magnetic energy. Wolverine was heading for a brick wall, but a gust of wind carried him to a safe landing.

"Much appreciated," he called up to Storm. She was riding the winds, heading for Magneto.

"No problem," she said. She rained a series of lightning blasts at Magneto, who repelled them with his magnetic force. Then Storm hurled Wolverine at him on a mighty gust of wind. Wolverine's razor-sharp claws were extended in front of him as he sped toward his foe.

But he hit an invisible wall of magnetic force and bounced off it, stunned.

"You truly have never understood the extent of my power," Magneto said.

"I guess I'm just stupid," Wolverine said. "Too stupid to know better." He leaped at Magneto again.

The master of magnetism raised his hand, and Wolverine froze in mid-leap, hanging in the air like some modern art display.

Storm flew close to Magneto, desperate to help Wolverine. But Magneto raised his other hand and sent her shooting away into the night sky. He focused his attention back on Wolverine.

"When will you learn your lesson?" Magneto asked. He was using his powers on Wolverine's metallic skeleton, stretching it.

Wolverine screamed in pain.

"Now, let's see," Magneto said, "if I can extract your skeleton from your flesh." And he started to do just that. Wolverine's howls of agony sounded like nothing human.

Suddenly, as if out of nowhere, there was a great rush of unleashed energy—energy that grew in force as it moved. It hit Magneto and sent him flying through a wall.

Wolverine fell to the ground and looked toward the source of the energy blast.

Jean Grey hovered in the air a few feet away.

24

Wolverine moved cautiously toward Jean. "Nice to see you," he said.

"Nice to see you, too," she replied.

Wolverine allowed himself to hope that Jean might come back to the X-Men. She had saved him. Maybe she could somehow make up for what she'd done. The professor would have liked that, in spite of everything.

But Wolverine's fantasy was just a fantasy. Another batch of U.S. military soldiers had arrived. They knew Jean had been with Magneto's army. They opened fire on her with mortar blasts.

Instinctively, she deflected them, but the force of the explosions knocked her back. Her physical self was unharmed—but the rage within her was again unleashed.

Rising into the sky, her energy spiraled out in all directions. It consumed walls and buildings, trees and tanks. It rippled out across the bay, illuminating the night.

In San Francisco, people saw the sky glowing, a strange new sun turning night into day. Gravity was going wild. People and objects were floating off the ground; others were sinking through the pavement.

And on the island of Alcatraz, the sky pulsed. It turned into a ball of fire. Then the flames started curling out from the center. They looked like the wings of a majestic, giant bird—like a phoenix.

And in the center of the flames was Jean. With each passing second, her flames burned brighter and hotter. Arcs of energy were shooting off of her, tearing Alcatraz to shreds.

"Get everybody off the island," Wolverine called to the X-Men. He started toward Jean.

Storm came up behind him. "You can't stop her alone," she said. "Let me help."

"I'm the only one who has a chance," he said. "We both know that."

Storm knew he was right. "Come back safe," she said to him. Then she hurried to assist the rest of the team.

Iceman had grabbed Pyro. Colossus had Leech. Warren Worthington Sr. had his son. Humans and mutants were working together to get off the island. Survival was the first order of business. Their differences could wait for another day.

But Magneto was nowhere to be found. Whether he was alive or dead, no one could say.

Jean's energy kept growing, ripping the island apart. The building and the supplies of the cure inside it were reduced to atoms.

Wolverine struggled against the telekinetic storm, trying to get closer to Jean.

"There's still a way to save you, Jean," he said.

"I don't need saving," she replied. "*You* do."

As he got closer, he felt the full fury of her power. His molecules started to speed up. Like Cyclops and Xavier, his flesh started to dissolve.

But Wolverine's mutant healing power kept him from their fate—at least for now. His skin kept rebuilding itself as fast as it decomposed.

Enraged by this, Jean erupted with even more energy. The earth beneath her shook, dissolving from her surge of power.

But Wolverine kept coming at her. Over and over, the process repeated itself: his skin dissolved and healed, dissolved and healed. In agony the entire time, he kept moving closer to her.

At last, he stood mere inches from her. Their eyes locked. She was in awe of her former teammate's bravery.

"You would die for them—for the people who would kill us just for being different?" she asked.

"Not for them," he said. "For you, Jean. For you."

Wolverine raised his arms. The claws popped out of the backs of his hands. All the while, his skin was dissolving around the blades. Jean's power had become too much for his healing power to resist. The end was drawing near.

Then something changed in Jean's eyes. For a moment, they softened.

"Save me," she whispered.

Wolverine embraced her. He kissed her one last

time. Then he leaned forward and ran a claw through the Phoenix.

Like Professor Xavier had once done, Wolverine had chosen the lesser evil. He had chosen to kill someone he loved in order to save the world.

As the life flowed out of her, the Phoenix became, for this one last moment, the Jean Grey that Wolverine had known and loved. Her lips formed a weak smile.

And then she was gone.

Wolverine collapsed to the ground, exhausted. He looked around at the ravaged island, now suddenly calm. His flesh was slowly healing itself. But he had never felt so physically and emotionally drained. Tears welled up in his eyes.

He finally got to his feet.

He lifted Jean's lifeless body into his arms and started walking to the bridge.

25

Wolverine stood at the bar, looking at old photographs. There were pictures from the many eras that made up his life. He lingered longest on a recent one. It was a shot of him and Jean with their arms around each other. They were laughing.

"Hey, I remember you," the bartender said.

"Yeah?" Wolverine replied. He remembered the bartender, too. The last time they met hadn't been pleasant. The man was a mutant-hater then.

The bartender slid a mug of beer over to him. "On the house," he said.

Wolverine raised an eyebrow. "What's the catch?" he asked.

"No catch," the man said. "I saw what you did. You saved everybody. The least that gets you is a free beer."

Wolverine put the photos into a dented metal box, then slid it across the counter. "Hold on to this for a few minutes, will you?" he said. "I'm on now." The bartender took the box and placed it under the bar.

Wolverine stripped off his jacket and headed back into a familiar cage. Bare-knuckled fighting wasn't the same as saving the world. But the rules were a lot clearer. And it sure was easier to tell the good guys from the bad guys.

The announcer's voice boomed through the bar's sound system. "Put your hands together," he said, "for the one, the only . . .

". . . Wolverine!"

The crowd went wild.

In Westchester, a new semester was beginning at the School for Gifted Youngsters.

Inside the professor's old office, Storm was speaking with Dr. Henry McCoy. "I'm going to need your help, Hank," she said. "We're going to have to figure out how to run this place without the professor."

"Happy to do anything I can," Hank replied. "I thought I might teach, oh, I don't know—history, maybe third-period Latin."

"Sounds good." She laughed. "You might want to do the occasional Danger Room session, too. Rumor has it some young mutants might be attending the school."

The two left the office and walked into the hall. Iceman, Colossus, Kitty, and Warren were waiting for them. Together, the X-Men walked down the corridor and opened the front door.

In the driveway, on the lawn, and spilling out into the road, were countless cars. They were filled with young mutants and their families. Thanks to the X-Men, more and more parents were no longer ashamed or afraid of their mutant children. The school was no longer a secret. It was a safe haven in a world that was changing.

Charles Xavier's dream was alive and well. And it was in excellent hands.